↑

?

Enjoy!

Lucy

Published by Brilliant Monsters Books
Brilliant Monsters Ltd, Registered Office:
15 Carew Road, London W13 9QL

First published 2021

001

Text Lucy Noguera
Text copyright Lucy Noguera
Illustrations Laura Ireland
Illustrations copyright Ai Ltd
Creative Director Finbar Lenahan, Ai
Cover Design Fabio Gois, Ai
Typeset Hazel Thomson, Ai
Proofreading Vanessa Harris

The moral right of the author and the illustrator has been asserted

Printed and Bound in the UK

MIX
Paper from
responsible sources
FSC® C020471

This book is a work of fiction. Names, characters, places, incidents, and
dialogues are products of the author's imagination or are used fictitiously.
Any resemblance to actual people, living or dead, events or locales is
entirely coincidental.

A CIP catalogue record for this book will be available
from the British Library

www.brilliantmonsters.com

ISBN 978-1-9145770-0-0

Ebook ISBN 978 -1-9145770-1-7

SWÖP

THE SATSUMA-SIZED SECRET

LUCY NOGUERA

ILLUSTRATED BY LAURA IRELAND

To Anthony, my husband,
I really couldn't have done
this without you!

DAD

MUM

ERNIE

THE TARGETT FAMILY

IVY

GRAN

Rafa

Ernie

Mr Mallon

Clemmie

CHAPTER 1

The Big Move

Ernie sighed and looked around his new bedroom, his heart thumping. His head was full of confusing emotions. This didn't seem real. How could this new house be his home when his dad wasn't there to share it?

Nothing felt familiar. There was a stack of cardboard boxes piled up against the wall with Ernie's name scribbled on them. Ivy, his fourteen-year-old sister, had labelled and drawn on all the

boxes. It was her way of "helping" without actually having to do any lifting or packing.

He looked at his bedside table. It was next to the bed where he always woke up but now they were both under a different ceiling. This one sloped and had wooden beams. It was in the loft, and now Ernie looked out of the window at all the other rooftops; so many families so close by and all in tall houses like this one.

He thought back to the view he'd had from his old bedroom window, of a quiet country lane and half of Mr David's garden, with his chicken run and falling-down shed.

Ernie wasn't thrilled about his new life, not at all. Although he had to admit it was nice to see his mum smiling and excited about working again and starting her new job as a doctor. Ivy was sometimes happy about moving to London and sometimes not, but that was Ivy. She was always changing her mind about things. Mum said it was because she was a teenager, but Ernie didn't see what that had to do with changing your mind a lot. Mum and Ivy were both downstairs now, opening boxes and laughing. He wasn't ready to go downstairs just yet. He didn't want to spoil their mood.

So, instead, he turned to look at the photo on the table by his bed. It was the only thing that was already unpacked. His mum must have done that. He stared at his dad's smiling face. Something his gran had said after his dad had died had stuck in his head. She told him he could still tell his dad all the things he wanted to, and he would just know what his dad would think or say back — because he knew his dad, just like his dad knew him, and that if Ernie did that, then his dad would never be far away.

Ernie knew that Gran wanted to believe the same thing because dad was her son, and he knew how much she missed him too. So, Ernie

decided to listen to Gran and give it a try. Now it was just something they always did, just like how he knew to look both ways when he crossed the road.

"Well, Dad, I'm here. We've arrived in London and moved everything in. So, now what do I do?" Ernie said in his head.

"You just need to unpack and make yourself at home!" responded imaginary Dad.

"Hmmm," Ernie mumbled to himself,

unimpressed by the answer.

He knew Dad had always looked on the bright side but today Ernie wasn't in the mood to listen.

"Come on, Ernie, my son. You never know, you might actually like your new bedroom." His dad's voice was still in his head.

Ernie squeezed his lips together tightly and turned his back on the photo. He wasn't sure he wanted this advice! Just as he did so, he thought he heard something. He listened carefully. There it was again, a tiny scuffling sound. So quiet he had to really listen to hear it. He sat very still. Maybe it was a bird on the roof, or a lawnmower outside, but then he heard it again and it was definitely coming from inside the house. He looked around his new bedroom — what could it be?

CHAPTER 2

The Memory Case

The noise stopped as quickly as it had started, so Ernie shrugged and half-heartedly opened the box labelled "Animal Books". He remembered his dad taking him to the bookshop to spend some birthday money a couple of years ago. Ernie had chosen a book about dogs and how to train them. He'd been so excited, mostly because his dad had promised him that when Ernie was older, they could get a puppy and train it together, but his dad had died not long after and that had been the end of that. Now Ernie flicked through the well-read pages, thinking about which kind of dog he liked best. He heard a laugh and a shriek from the floor below. Ivy and Mum were obviously having fun.

He couldn't help feeling a little jealous of Ivy sometimes. She made friends easily. She was deaf, so she used sign language with her friends or closely watched people's lips when they spoke to her, which meant she was always right in the thick of things, in the middle of people. Ernie often felt like he was the complete opposite, always on the outside looking in. His mum's voice calling up the stairs broke his thoughts.

"Ernie, what are you doing? Are you OK? Shall we come up and help you?" Her voice was faint, only just reaching up the extra flights of stairs.

He sat up straight and shouted back in his most convincing voice towards the open door, "Yep, yep all fine, Mum. No thanks, I'll be down soon, just, er, planning out my new room!"

"OK. We're having fish and chips with Gran tonight. I'll let you know when she gets here," Mum answered.

It was nice that they lived so close to Gran now, but Ernie still couldn't help feeling it was a tiny bit unfair that the three of them had had to move to be near her (although he would never admit that because he really loved Gran). It was just that there was only one of Gran – so surely it would have been easier if she'd moved to be near them?

He stood up, sighed and looked around for his memory box. That would cheer him up. It was really just an old suitcase but it was full of all his most precious possessions. He spotted it on the floor beside the book boxes. That wasn't good. It shouldn't have been taken out of its packing. Ernie had triple-checked the latches before they left but now the case was unlocked and its lid ajar.

Everyone in his family knew not to open Ernie's case. It was very private. It wasn't much to look at, just a battered old brown leather suitcase, its lid once stamped in bright gold with the initials he shared with his dad, his grandad, and an alien from one of his dad's favourite 80s movies: ET. He was Ernie Targett, his dad was Eric Targett and his grandad was Ernest Targett. Now the letters were faded like the colours of an old photograph.

Still puzzled, Ernie lifted the case carefully

onto his bed, and as he did so, he heard the same scurrying sound he'd heard earlier. Was something moving around inside it? He quickly shoved the case away and jumped back. The noise stopped. He looked around and listened hard but the room was silent. Then a little "yip, yip, yip" noise came from the case. Something was definitely in there! Had someone put an old toy inside when they were packing?

The noise came again, slightly louder this time: "Yap yap yip!" That was no toy — that was the sound of a real creature! What if it was nibbling on his treasure or, worse, weeing on all his special certificates? Ernie stepped forwards, leant across the bed, flung the lid back and looked in, heart thumping.

Nothing.

The inside of the case looked like it always did — a jumbled-up collection of treasure: paper, rocks, marbles, certificates, stickers and, the most recent addition, a twig. The twig was from a tree in the park, the one he would climb while his dad sat on the bench underneath, waiting for him. Ernie had gone to find the tree before they left. It had been a while since he had visited and he was surprised by how small the tree looked now. He'd picked up a little twig from beneath it and popped it in his pocket.

Ernie sat on his bed, took off one of his

trainers and used it to prod at the treasure pile. He rolled a white pebble from Brighton beach to one side to see if there was anything underneath it. Still nothing. Then the corner of his map of the Natural History Museum, (otherwise known as his favourite place on Earth) flicked up, just the tiniest bit. Quickly and clumsily,

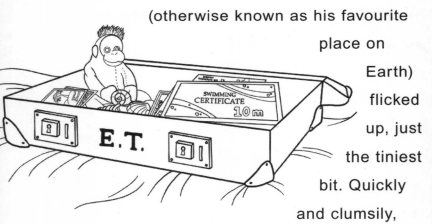

Ernie used his trainer to flip it over and there, beneath the map, next to a very dirty lucky penny, was a small black-and-white ball of hair.

Ernie leapt back and yelled, "Argh! What's that?"

A tiny face with chestnut brown eyes and a wet black nose appeared out of the fur.

13

The pocket-sized creature seemed to be as surprised to see Ernie as Ernie was to see it. It gave a little shake and then stood up, ears pricked. It had four tiny legs and a fluffy tail that started to move — no, to wag...

It was a dog! A tiny but absolutely and most definitely real dog!

CHAPTER 3

🐾

The Best Treasure of All

Ernie stared, his mouth open. He couldn't believe what he was seeing. The tiny dog started to whine, then looked straight at Ernie and quickly clambered up over his treasures, desperate to get to him. Instinctively, Ernie bent down and held out his hand, and as he did so the little dog took a leap and with a warm, soft thump landed right in the middle of Ernie's palm.

This was a real living dog, and yet it was smaller than a tennis ball, smaller than an orange — in fact, it was more like one of those little easy-to-peel oranges... yes, that was it, it was satsuma-sized! Ernie's grin was so wide that his cheeks hurt. He tilted his head to look at the little dog and it copied him, its tongue poking out of the side of its mouth to show it was concentrating. Ernie laughed out loud. His memory box always made him smile but this was something else!

"Hello! Who are you, then?" he whispered excitedly.

Ernie was worried he was dreaming and that he would wake up and find the little dog had disappeared. He put the back of his other hand in front of the dog's nose. Its breath felt very real on his skin. The dog sniffed his hand once but he already seemed to know that Ernie wasn't a threat. It reminded Ernie of when a duckling attaches itself to the first person it sees when it hatches out of its shell.

The little dog looked as if it were almost

smiling at Ernie, its eyes tiny, dark and friendly, the size and colour of apple pips. Ernie lifted the little dog right up in front of his face, just like how the BFG lifted Sophie up in Ernie's favourite Roald Dahl book. As Ernie studied the little creature, it leapt forwards and licked his face! It was like having a wash with a tiny paintbrush, and it tickled so much that Ernie laughed and squirmed away. Then he stopped and the little dog stopped too, and they just looked at each other. Ernie grinned, he didn't need to pinch

17

himself, he definitely wasn't dreaming!

"Hey, hey! So, little fella — what are you doing hiding in my suitcase? I hope you haven't chewed anything." Ernie was just talking to himself — the dog wasn't listening, it was just jumping up and down, as excited as if it were about to go on a trip to a sausage shop.

Ernie gently stroked it from head to tail with one finger and found the dog's favourite tickle spot just behind its left ear. Every time Ernie stopped stroking it, the dog dipped its head towards him, encouraging him to carry on. Ernie's heart felt so full it might burst and he felt like he wanted to tell the whole world his good news. It had been a while since he'd felt this good. Ernie knew in an instant that this dog was meant for him. It didn't matter where it had come from, and it didn't matter why it had come. All that mattered was that they were together. This very tiny but absolutely perfect, scruffy black-and-white dog felt like a little piece of Ernie that he hadn't even known was missing, slotting safely back into place like the last piece in a jigsaw puzzle.

"What kind of dog are you, then? You look a bit like a quite a few breeds. I'll need to get my dog book out and look you up. Although I'm pretty sure I haven't seen a dog quite like you before! Are you the only one this small? You're full of beans too, so you must be a puppy!" The dog wasn't magic, it couldn't answer but it wagged his tail hard, so Ernie knew it was happy and that was enough for now.

Suddenly, Ernie realised everything had changed. He no longer had to pretend to be excited about moving to London – he actually was excited! He scooped up the little pup with one hand, holding the other hand cupped over the top to keep it safe, then turned for the door, desperate to run downstairs and show his mum and sister what he'd found, but as he reached the bedroom door, he came to his senses and skidded to a halt. Only yesterday he'd had to give away Sticky, his beloved stick insect, to his best friend Max. What was he thinking? The letter the landlord had stuck through their letterbox flashed in his mind. It said, "No Pets Allowed" in big bold letters, and in tiny capitals underneath, "*I mean it! Not even a goldfish!"

If he wasn't even allowed to bring Sticky here then there was no way he'd be allowed to keep a real, live dog, even if it was a satsuma-sized one. He couldn't risk it. This was meant to be. He had always wanted a dog and now his dream had come true. The most perfect dog he had ever seen had found him! There was only one answer. If he wanted to keep the dog, Ernie was going to have to keep it a secret.

CHAPTER 4

🐾

The Fastest Fish Supper

Ernie sat at the breakfast bar barely noticing their new kitchen, although he had to admit the high bar stools were quite cool and if he weren't in such a hurry to get back upstairs he would definitely have enjoyed spinning around on them. There would be time for that on another day. Instead, he squibbed far too much ketchup on his plate and then ate his fish and chips so fast he hardly tasted them.

Ivy was shaking her head and pulling disgusted faces at him. She even signed the word "Pig" but Ernie just nodded, smiling back

with his cheeks bulging. He signed "Thank you!" at her. He was too happy to argue with his sister, even though normally it was something he enjoyed, in fact it was a bit like a hobby — but not today.

"Ernie, slow down, you'll make yourself sick!" His mum said, surprised by his scoffing.

"S'OK, I'm just starving, and I really want to

get back upstairs to, er... unpack," answered
Ernie with his mouth full.

"But your gran has only just arrived. Surely
your unpacking can wait a few more minutes?"
Mum was raising one eyebrow and giving him
her special "mum look".

"Oh, it's OK, Ernest. You eat up, you're a
growing boy," said Gran. "When your dad was

your age, he was for ever in the fridge!" She smiled at Ernie with such kindness it gave him a little stab of guilt in his stomach. He looked at her plate. She had only eaten about three chips and hadn't even touched her fish yet.

"I tell you what," continued Gran. "How about you head back upstairs in a minute and then, when we've all finished our tea, I'll climb up those stairs and come and see how you're getting along, shall I?" Ernie froze. He couldn't risk Gran seeing the little dog in his bedroom.

"It's OK, Gran," answered Ernie, a little too quickly. "I want to finish my room properly before you see it."

"Ernie!" said Mum sharply, unable to keep the annoyance out of her voice.

Gran winked at him, "It's OK, Ernest love, I understand. And you'll be seeing a lot more of me now we live so close, so there's no rush."

Ernie felt hot as his face flushed. He was

sure he was as red as the ketchup he had managed to smear all over his hands in his haste. He didn't mean to be rude to his gran, but he was just so desperate to make sure he hadn't just invented the whole incredible miniature dog incident.

Ivy mouthed "Rude boy" at him at the same time as signing it, then swivelled around dramatically on her stool, turning her back on him. He looked down at his plate and promised himself he'd make it up to Gran soon. Gran had turned her attention to Ivy now, careful to make sure that Ivy could read her lips, and was asking her about her new school. Mum was signing alongside Gran so that Ivy could understand everything Gran was asking. Gran was learning how to sign but needed some practice. Ernie used this distraction to get up and speedily rinse his plate. He could feel Mum's eyes on him as he crossed the kitchen and then ran up the stairs as fast as his legs could carry him.

He swung open the bedroom door and then pushed it shut, shoving one of his book boxes against it to make sure it stayed shut. His heart seemed to be beating so loudly he was sure the little dog would hear it — that's if it was still there... Ernie bent down beside his bed and pulled out his dad's old black beanie hat, and there, exactly where he had left him but now fast asleep, all curled up like a dormouse, was the little dog!

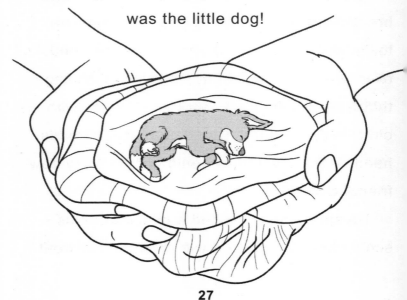

CHAPTER 5

Ernie's New Best Friend

Ernie lifted the hat carefully on to his bed, the little dog still sleeping soundly inside it. Then he lay back on his bed and took a huge breath. In just one day he had swapped one town for another, one home for another, and even one pet for another. He loved swapping things. He would miss swapping comics with his old friends. Suddenly an idea flashed into his head — that's what he would call his furry new friend: Swap!

He sat up and grabbed a pencil from his school box. He wrote Swap down on the front of his book box, then shook his head — it just didn't look right. He tried it again, this time in capital letters: SWAP. Nope – it just didn't look like a name. Then he changed the "a" to an "o". That worked much better. An unusual name for a very unusual little dog!

So Swop it was.

The little dog soon became Ernie's best friend. He was so titchy he could fit into Ernie's hand or hide easily in his pocket, but the best thing about him was that he wasn't imaginary, he wasn't a toy, he was real — a living, breathing, walking 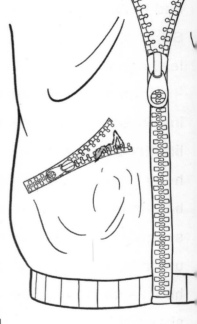 and barking dog, who just happened to be the size of a satsuma. And no-one in Ernie's family, not even his mum or his sister, knew anything about him — and Ernie knew he had to keep it that way.

One of the first things Ernie did was make Swop his own miniature dog house. He wanted Swop to have somewhere to play when Ernie had to leave him alone. It had to be cosy for Swop, but also make Ernie feel happy about leaving him.

Ernie had great fun making a play area inside an old shoebox. He built a slide and a little den, and added a mini bouncy ball that he smeared in peanut butter. He had tip-toed behind his mum in the kitchen and managed to scoop a spoonful out of the jar before running upstairs with it, just to keep Swop happy if he was going to be out for a few hours. The shoebox home even had real lights, a string of battery-powered fairy lights that Ivy had discarded during the move. There was a toilet corner covered in little pieces of newspaper and a little soft area for naps — although Ernie had already discovered that Swop preferred to sleep under his bed inside Ernie's dad's old beanie hat.

Swop also liked it best when one of Ernie's dirty socks was inside the beanie hat with him. It was the only way Ernie could get him to go to sleep at night and stop him crying. The sock smelt of Ernie, and Ernie knew that dogs like to have something close by that smells of their

SWOP'S HOUSE!

human. Swop would settle down in the hat when Ernie went to bed and as long as Ernie stayed in bed, Swop would stay in the hat too. Ernie couldn't trust Swop to keep hidden if he left him in the hat when he went out, so instead he made sure that the little dog was safe inside his shoebox house and had plenty to keep him busy.

Ernie and his family had moved during the summer holidays to give them time to settle into their new area before the school term started, so Ernie had a few clear weeks to get to know his new friend. But then what would he do? His head was swimming with questions and ideas. He knew he would have to work fast and hope that Swop was a quick learner. He wanted to keep this dog and he knew that was going to take serious planning and dedication. In his head he imagined his dad smiling down at him, telling him he could do it, that he would think of

a way to train Swop and keep him safe
and happy.

Ernie nodded quietly to himself, wondering
if his dad could see him or knew about Swop.
Swop was here for a reason, he was sure of it.
And even though he knew things were going to
be tricky once he had to be at school all day,
Ernie was ready to rise to the challenge.

CHAPTER 6

The Puppy Poo Parcels

Ernie woke up before his alarm clock rang. His first thought every morning now was Swop. Today, his second thought was that it was Monday. It was the first day at his new school. He threw his quilt to one side and swung his head down to look under the bed. It was so tidy under there. In his old house he'd had Lego, odd socks and hidden biscuit wrappers shoved underneath his bed — they'd needed two large bin-bags to clear it all when they moved. Now all he could see was his dad's old upside-down hat with a couple of his own dirty socks inside.

Usually Swop was still curled up in it each morning when Ernie looked but today, the hat was empty...

He scanned the room — he didn't have to look far. Swop was standing next to Ernie's shiny school shoes, sniffing them. Ernie opened his mouth to say hello but before any words came out, Swop lifted up his back leg and weed in a perfect arc, all down the side of Ernie's left shoe.

"Swop! No!" he called out through gritted teeth.

It was too late. Swop was mid-stream and couldn't stop, but he still turned and ran towards Ernie, leaving a teeny spotty trail of wee all across the wooden floor.

"Ewwwwww, Swop!"

Ernie jumped out of bed and sat on the floor so Swop could climb up on to him. The little dog reached him in a second. He was very excited this morning, climbing and licking Ernie and making his happy noise, a little yip, yip, yip.

"Ernie, time for breakfast! You need to come down now — are you dressed yet? It's seven fifteen, come on, hurry up!" Mum's voice sounded far away but was loud enough to make Ernie panic.

He tore off his pyjamas and threw on his brand-new navy blue school uniform, which he'd laid out on a chair the night before. Then he yanked on his socks, clipped on his tie and reached for his shoes. Ewww! He could still see wee down the side. He looked around for something to wipe it off. Ernie was quickly learning that being a dog owner wasn't all fun and games. He grabbed a sock from Swop's bed, and pulled a face as he quickly dried and polished the shoe, then cleaned up the tiny wee trail on the wooden floor before flinging the now very yucky sock into the laundry basket.

He ran to the door but as he got there he felt something pinching and pulling at the bottom of his trouser leg. Swop was hanging off the hem of his trousers by his teeth. He'd forgotten to put the little dog back in his cardboard box apartment.

"Swop! Get off. You know you can't come down to breakfast, everyone will see you!" Ernie said firmly.

He bent down and gently pulled Swop off his leg, then popped him in the cardboard box and shut the bedroom door carefully as he went downstairs. When Ernie came back up after breakfast, he'd smuggled a few cornflakes in his pocket for Swop.

"OK, just this once you can eat in my pocket and come with me into the bathroom while I clean my teeth, since I won't see you for most of the day," Ernie said as he looked at Swop. He signed "Quiet" and popped the dog into his pocket.

Ernie cleaned his teeth at the basin, then lifted Swop out again. The little dog's face was covered in cornflake crumbs. Ernie took a milk carton lid from his pocket and half-filled it with water and put it on the edge of the sink. Swop sniffed it, then stuck his head in and quickly lapped up the water. Teeny splashes went all over the place. Swop stopped and looked up at him; he now had a soggy mess of water and cornflake crumbs on his face, which had made his fur go all pointy, so it looked like he had a tiny goat's beard. Water was dripping off the pointy bit, so Ernie turned to get some toilet paper to wipe Swop's face.

When he turned back, Swop was crouched on the edge of the sink, about to do a poo. Swop had got quite good at using the little newspaper toilet area Ernie had made for him in his shoebox, but he clearly hadn't used it yet this morning. Ernie quickly tore off a corner of toilet paper and held it under Swop's tiny bum — Plop! Plop! Just in time he caught two ladybird-sized parcels of puppy poo in his hand! Ernie knew he was still a puppy and had some way to go before he was completely accident-free. He was just pleased that Swop's poo's were so tiny!

Ernie held his nose, screwing up his

face, then scrunched the paper and dropped the little poo parcel into the toilet and flushed it away, washing his hands afterwards. Swop just looked at him and wagged his tail.

Ernie shook his head. "Ha! Don't think I am going to be doing that forever!" he said, laughing.

"ERNNNNIIEEE! You need to come down, now!

It's twenty-five to eight, time for school,"
Mum's voice reminded him, as though he didn't
actually know how to tell the time.

Ernie sighed, scooped Swop up and hurried
out of the bathroom. His stomach was doing
back flips. The idea of walking in to a new
school and a new class was making him feel
a bit sick... He took Swop back to the shoebox
house. He was thinking about school and in a
hurry, so for the first time ever, he didn't
quite close the lid properly after he popped
Swop inside.

"See you later, Swop. Wish me luck!" Ernie
said, tapping the cardboard house twice
for good luck, then bending down to tie his
shoelaces. He straightened up, swung his
half-open school bag over his shoulder, and
hurried out, waving behind him as he went.
Unfortunately, he wasn't the only one to leave
the room that morning...

CHAPTER 7

The Leaping Lunchbox

Ernie joined the rest of his class as they lined up in the playground, his head buzzing with questions. Would they be a friendly class? Would he make any friends? Would the maths be harder than at his last school? Where were the toilets? He was trying really hard to just focus on the awesome packed lunch his mum had made him, even though it wasn't long since he'd had breakfast. Gran had left one of her famous cupcakes for him to take too. It wasn't easy being the new kid and his nerves were making his stomach swirl his breakfast around.

Then he heard a very familiar voice behind him calling his name.

"Yoo hoo, Ernie? Ernest, Ernie, it's me!" It was Gran and she was moving up the line to get to him. The embarrassment made Ernie freeze on the spot, his hopes of blending in and being unnoticed evaporating. His stomach sank as Mr Mallon strode past him to intercept Gran.

"Hello, how can I help you? I'm Ernie's teacher, Mr Mallon."

"Oh, it's so nice to meet you! I'm Ernie's granny. His mum said he'd forgotten his lunch so I've brought it in for him."

Mr Mallon smiled. "That is very kind of you. He's over there. You're just in time!" he said, pointing at Ernie.

Ernie gritted his teeth, then turned around slowly with a pasted-on smile that on the outside said how happy he was to see his granny in the playground in front of all his new

classmates — and on the inside said, "Please, please, let a huge hole in the ground open up and take me back in time to when I left the lunchbox behind and let me remember to pick it up!"

"Here you go, my love," said Gran, grinning. Her glasses were huge and bright blue, which

also matched all her jewellery. She had an old
camera around her neck. She didn't like to use
a phone camera. Ernie prayed she wasn't going
to take a picture of him starting his new school.
That would be just the kind of thing she would
do. He sighed. She was one of those people
everyone loved, which meant that whoever was

with her got noticed too — which was fine if you were Ivy but not fine if you were Ernie.

Gran triumphantly waved Ernie's ancient Star Wars lunch box in the air, like it was a prize. Ernie blushed as he took the rusty tin.

"Thank you," he squeaked. He was so embarrassed even his toes felt hot. He took an extra step back just in case Gran flung her arms around him. Luckily, she didn't. Ernie thought he would tell his dad about this scene when he had his usual chat with his dad at bedtime. As Gran was dad's mum, he and Ernie had always laughed about all the things she got up to.

"Goodbye, Mrs Targett. Next time just pop it in the office," said Mr Mallon, as he waved the children into class.

"Of course!" Gran did a sideways nod and winked at Ernie as she patted him twice on the shoulder.

"Hmmm," thought Ernie, raising one eyebrow. "Good luck with that." Gran had never been much of a rule follower. Gran headed off, waving dramatically to the other children, bracelets jangling as she went.

The rest of the morning passed uneventfully and both hands on the clock were finally almost at 12, meaning it would soon be lunchtime — at last. Ernie's mouth was watering at the thought of the fantastic cupcake he had in his packed lunch today. Gran might be embarrassing but she was the best baker ever!

The bell finally rang and the children were sent in to lunch, one table at a time to prevent a stampede. Ernie's newly allocated lunch buddy, Rafa, was already chomping away before his bum had even hit the seat. Ernie sat down beside him and took out his lunchbox. As he lifted the lid, Rafa asked, mouth full, "What

sandwiches have you got?" But before Ernie
could answer...

Splitter, splatter, splosh!

A jet of strawberry yoghurt squirted out of
Ernie's lunchbox and hit him straight in the
face. Ernie gasped, wobbling backwards on
his chair before righting himself and slamming
down the metal lunchbox lid. His eyes crossed
as a blob of strawberry yoghurt slowly slid
down his nose and plopped on to the table-top.

Ernie gulped as he wiped his sticky lashes with his fingers. Had Rafa noticed? Oh dear... yes... he had. Rafa's mouth was wide open, a lump of mushed-up bread and cheese on display for all to see.

"Ernie! What. On. Earth. Just. Happened?" Rafa was laughing as he pointed at Ernie's sticky pink face. "Looked like your lunch box just attacked you!"

"Er, I have no idea. I... I must have just slammed the lid on a yoghurt. Er... and lost my balance, the chair must be broken," stuttered Ernie.

A noise made them both turn round. The lunchbox was rattling on the table. Rafa bent down and looked underneath the table to see if anyone was moving it. Ernie looked too.

"What are you two boys doing over there?" shouted Mrs Grumble, the lunch supervisor. "Sit up straight now!" Her voice was sharp and

the two boys jumped as if they had been poked with a pin!

There was a group of girls from their class on the table behind them, and they all turned to stare. One of them, Clemmie, saw that Ernie was looking upset so she distracted the other girls and stopped them laughing at him. Ernie got the feeling she'd sensed his embarrassment when he'd arrived in their class that morning because she'd gone out of her way to make him feel welcome ever since. Mrs Grumble glared at the boys once more before turning on her pointy heels to find her next victim.

"Ernie, what happened?" asked Clemmie quietly, leaning across.

"Er, nothing," he mumbled.

"The lunchbox just attacked him," said Rafa, laughing.

"Good one, Rafa," said Clemmie, sighing. "Seriously, though, are you OK, Ernie? Do you want me to get the other supervisor?" Her face showed her concern. "He's really nice, if you do need anything." Ernie managed a tiny smile, and shook his head. Clemmie smiled and turned back to her pasta salad.

"Why did this have to happen today, of all days?" Ernie thought to himself, as he wiped his eyes directly on the sleeve of his new jumper. It looked like he wasn't going to be having the uneventful first day at LK Primary he'd hoped for.

CHAPTER 8

The Secret Den

Clatter... clatter

Ernie's eyes were now clear enough of strawberry yoghurt to spot that the lunchbox was wiggling again. He lunged for it before anyone else noticed it moving. He gritted his teeth and held on for dear life.

"H...eeelllppp!" whispered Ernie, staring straight at Rafa.

Rafa looked up. He realised his new friend wasn't mucking around and frowned. Ernie seemed to be on the verge of tears as he struggled to keep his lunchbox still. Ernie swivelled his eyes towards the lunchbox lid and suddenly Rafa saw what was making his friend act so strangely. Something black and white and fluffy was poking out of the corner of the lid where it wasn't closed properly — and it was moving! Was it alive? Or a toy of some kind? Rafa stared. Then he saw something that looked like a leg begin to edge its way out of the lunchbox.

Before he had a chance to work out quite what he was seeing, Ernie quickly but carefully pushed it back inside the lunchbox and closed the lid. Luckily it was noisy in the hall. No one was watching. So Rafa grabbed Ernie and the misbehaving lunchbox, being careful not to tip whatever was inside out.

"Ernie, come on. I know where we can go!" Rafa said confidently. There was something about Rafa's face that made Ernie want to trust him. He nodded.

"Right, follow me!" Rafa said, already on his feet and weaving between the chaotic lunchtime tables, pulling his new friend towards the door. Ernie kept close behind. A few shouts

of "Oi!" and "Rafa!" rang across the room as the two boys bashed into the back of a chair or two, but nobody stopped them, and at last they burst out through the canteen doors and into the playground. The two of them crossed the playground. Ernie felt nervous. Rafa was practically a stranger — could he trust him? He had a feeling he could, but what if he was wrong? They arrived at a huge row of dense bushes on the edge of the playground. Rafa turned, smiled and beckoned to Ernie. Then suddenly he wasn't there!

Ernie looked around. He couldn't see Rafa but spotted a gap in the hedge, so he ducked down and climbed right into the bush. It was amazing inside, opening out into what felt like a leafy igloo. The sun filtered through the leaves and made streams of light, swirling with specks of gold. On the ground were two seats made out of an upturned bucket and an old plastic milk crate. In the middle was a chunk of tree trunk that looked like someone had been using it as a table. Rafa was there waiting and he gestured at the upturned bucket as if it were a throne.

"Welcome to my totally secret den, my new friend, you and your energetic packed lunch are most welcome!" Ernie was frozen to the spot.

"Oh come on, Ernie, move yourself! I want to find out what's going on. What's inside the box?" said Rafa, starting to get impatient now. "Or maybe it's who is inside the box?"

Ernie took a deep breath and gently put the lunchbox on the table. "OK, Rafa... it is a who. Can you definitely keep a secret?"

Rafa grinned. "Yes, of course, I was born to keep secrets. This den is a secret! I am the king of secrets. Now come on, before the bell goes again. Can I open it, what is it? A mouse, an alien... an alien mouse?!" Rafa grabbed a long stick from the ground, then looked at Ernie for permission. Ernie nodded and watched Rafa flip up the lid of his lunchbox — stepping back as he did so.

They both waited... And... nothing.

"Wait, Rafa, leave it a second. Perhaps he's scared." Rafa was now the one looking worried.

"Who?"

"OK, watch, I'll show you... Just remember, you gave me your word."

Rafa put his hand over his heart, nodded and

said quietly, "I swear, Ernie, you have my word — unless it's a spider. I hate spiders!"

Ernie used his fingers to lift up the sticky crust of his ham sandwich, then moved the empty red rind of what had once been a small round of cheese. The yoghurt pot had been squashed and there were tiny teeth marks around the edges of everything. And there was the upturned wrapper from the cupcake he'd been looking forward to eating all morning... the squashed-up cupcake was spoilt and no longer inside the wrapper. Ernie groaned. The wrapper looked like it had something else inside it, although it was a bit of a strange shape. Rafa was peering over Ernie's

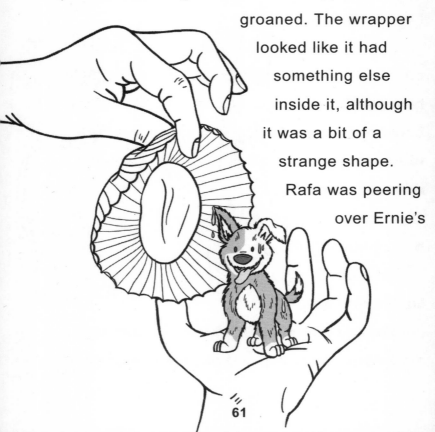

shoulder now, making sure Ernie was closer to the box than he was. Just as they both looked at the cake wrapper, it moved. In fact, it ran and scrambled over the bread crust and squeezed itself into the corner of the lunchbox. Rafa shrieked and leapt back.

"It's a tarantula, I saw its hairy feet! I knew it!"

Ernie could see Swop's black paws poking out from under the cake wrapper. He couldn't help but smile — they did look rather like they could be a tarantula's feet. There was a little tear in the wrapper too, so he could just see one teeny brown eye.

"It's definitely not a tarantula, Rafa. It's... well... it's just Swop!"

"W-w-wh-at is a Swop?" Rafa stuttered.

"Swop, come here," Ernie said with a sigh.

He was ready to share his secret — he just

had to hope Rafa was the right person to help him. The walking cake wrapper clambered over the side of the lunchbox and on to Ernie's outstretched hand.

"Ready, Rafa?" Like a magician revealing a bunny in a hat, Ernie lifted the wrapper into the air to reveal a very real, slightly wet and rather sticky satsuma-sized dog. "Rafa, meet Swop, Swop meet Rafa!"

CHAPTER 9

The Pom-Pom Puppy

Ernie carefully put Swop down on the tree trunk table in front of them and watched him licking his strawberry-flavoured paws. Ernie looked up nervously at Rafa but the butterflies in his stomach soon started to fly away because Rafa was grinning. Rafa crouched low and moved closer to Swop.

"Hello, little fella!" he whispered warmly. He started to put his hand out

but then pulled it back, looking at Ernie as if unsure what to do.

"Let him smell the back of your hand. It's the cleanest part of your body so it smells the most of you," reassured Ernie. Rafa gently put the back of his hand in front of the tiny sticky fluff ball.

"Wow, Ernie, he is just brilliant! Hello Swop, I'm Rafa. Lovely to meet you." Swop stopped licking and shuffled forward to sniff him.

"Stroke his head, just gently, between his ears with one finger. He loves that," said Ernie. Rafa did, and Swop rolled over onto his back, legs in the air. Rafa laughed and rubbed his belly as Swop wriggled around, ears dangling and tongue hanging out. Ernie's chest filled with pride, even though he knew this was risky. He had kept Swop a secret for weeks now. It was brilliant to finally get the chance to show him off to someone else.

"Rafa, I need you to listen. Swop is a secret. I can't let anyone know about him. We're not allowed pets in our house because our landlord hates pets. Mum said he would make us move out even if he found out we had a goldfish! Also Swop's so special I'm sure everyone would want him. He would be taken away from me. People would want to see him. He would become famous and valuable then people might try and steal him! So please, please, Rafa, you can't tell anyone. I mean it. No one!" Swop was still happily licking his paws. Rafa stood, looked Ernie straight in the eye and put his hand over

his heart.

"I solemnly swear that your secret is safe with me." He put his hand out to shake Ernie's. Ernie shook it firmly and then they both looked down at Swop and laughed. Swop was now sitting up straight, holding up one paw as if he wanted to shake hands too.

"Well, don't leave him hanging, it took almost two packets of ham to teach him that!" Ernie said, laughing. So Rafa knelt down and delicately but purposefully shook Swop's paw.

"Swop, I, Rafael Peréz, promise to help Ernie keep you safe." Rafa looked at his watch

— he knew they were running out of time and lunch break would soon be over, but he now had a mission: to be Swop's personal dog-guard! This den could be his and Ernie's secret meeting place. After all, every agent needs a base. And they needed it more than ever now, so he'd better make sure they weren't spotted coming out of it…

"OK, so what do we do next?" asked Rafa, standing up straight, ready for his instructions.

"First Swop and I need to get cleaned up — and then we need to decide what to do with him until it's time to go home. Let's go to the boys' toilets and give him a wash." Ernie picked up Swop, told him to stay, then popped him in his pocket. Then he closed up the empty lunchbox.

"Right," said Rafa, "Let's get going."

They headed off to the toilets with Swop bobbing up and down in Ernie's pocket, as he half-ran, half-walked across the playground, trying to keep up with Rafa while also trying not to attract any attention. Rafa seemed to be extremely excited by his new role. He barged open the toilet door, then crouched down to do a quick scan under the cubicle doors to see if he could spot any feet.

"All clear."

Relieved, Ernie thrust his hand into his pocket and pulled out Swop. Just then, the five-minute bell rang. BRRRRRRRRRing!!!! BRRRRRRRing!!!! BRRRRRRRRRing!!!! Lunchtime was almost over. They had to hurry.

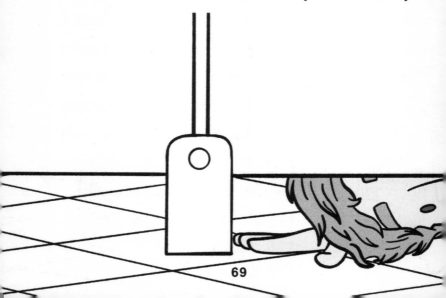

69

Rafa guarded the door as Ernie lifted Swop up high and brought him closer to his face. He had cake crumbs, a pencil shaving and bits of tissue stuck to his legs. His tiny tongue shot out and started licking Ernie's nose like it was an ice cream. Ernie giggled, but then his face turned serious.

"Stop it, Swop, I need you to behave! We have to get you sorted quickly!" He lowered his hand a bit so Swop couldn't reach his face for any more licking. "Swop, you know you were supposed to stay at home today."

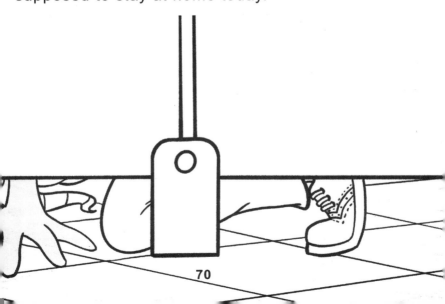

Swop looked down at his wet paws. His flattened his ears against his head and the corners of his shiny chestnut-brown eyes drooped. Ernie knew exactly what this meant. Swop was sorry. Ernie glanced at himself in the mirror. His face and fringe were still sticky.

Swop enjoyed his quick shower. Ernie gently cupped Swop in his hands (now looking like a baby chick just out of its shell) and held him under the dryer. Swop loved having the warm air blasting his fur back and forth. He turned his face upwards, which made his lips wobble – Drrrr Drrrr Drrrr – and showed off a mouthful of gleaming white miniature teeth. He was dry and fluffed back up in just a few seconds. Ernie showed him to Rafa.

"He looks just like the pom-pom on Clemmie's hat!" Rafa laughed.

The toilet door began to be pushed open from the outside. Ernie panicked and popped Swop just inside the neck of his jumper. He looked down and could see his little confused face peeping back up at him, his mouth slightly open. Ernie couldn't help but smile as Swop reminded him of a baby bird in a nest waiting for a juicy worm to be dropped in its mouth.

Clunk! Clank! Rafa had quickly pushed back against the door. The door was pushed back again from the other side.

"Who's in there?" said an angry and familiar voice. It was Josh. Rafa had already told Ernie that he was the meanest boy in their class. Ernie looked at Rafa in a panic, checking Swop

was comfy but out of sight inside his jumper, just in case Josh burst in.

"You can't come in, Josh, the toilets have overflowed," shouted Rafa. Ernie was once again impressed by new friend's quick thinking! "There's wee everywhere!"

"Why, what have you done, Rafa, had an accident? Ha, ha, I always knew you were a big baby!" shouted Josh through the door, annoyed that he couldn't come in.

"You're the baby," mumbled Rafa to himself. Josh gave the door a final kick and ran off. Luckily, he was nowhere near as strong as he wanted to be. Suddenly Ernie jumped.

"Ouch, Swop, stop it, behave!" Ernie was patting himself all over as if being stung by wasps, until a cheeky little face appeared over the neck of his jumper.

Rafa burst out laughing as Swop climbed out and bounded along Ernie's arm, giving his neck a quick nuzzle as he went. Swop stopped and gazed up at Ernie, his eyes bright and hopeful. Ernie smiled. He couldn't stay cross with Swop for long.

The bell went again. It really was time to get to class. Ernie knew he'd have to keep Swop quiet for the rest of the afternoon, but first he had to sort one thing out... Quickly he grabbed a paper hand-towel and placed it on the floor. It must have been ages since Swop had last been to the toilet.

"Do a wee, Swop, do a wee!" Swop slid off Ernie's hand and on to the floor. The little dog went straight over to the paper towel, cocked one leg and did a wee on the paper. Rafa looked impressed.

"Good boy," said Ernie, rolling up the paper and placing it in the bin. He scooped Swop back up and stroked his head.

"Woof, woof, woof, woof, woof!" barked Swop.

"Come on Swop, you need to be quiet!" Ernie whispered, as he signed "Quiet". It looked

like he was holding both ends of a piece of string together and then pulling them away from each other until they were straight. Ernie's sister Ivy had taught him some handy sign language and he had spent many hours, and shared numerous cheese-and-ham sandwiches, teaching Swop some of the key signs. Now Swop wagged his fluffy tail, which meant he understood.

"That's so cool," said Rafa. "What does it mean?"

"It means be quiet," said Ernie. "I can use signs to tell him silently what I need him to do, so it's a great way of warning

him about stuff without anyone else noticing.
Doesn't always mean he'll do what I've asked,
though – I'm still working on that bit. It works
better with a piece of cheese, but he's already
stuffed full from my lunch!" Swop started
jumping up Ernie, tail wagging as fast as if he
were a wind-up toy. He was getting excited.

"No, Swop, you must stay in my pocket and
you must be quiet!" Ernie said, signing again,
"Quiet and stay! Do you understand?"

"Woof, woof!"

Ernie and Rafa both stroked Swop's
head, then Ernie quickly slid Swop into
his trouser pocket.

"OK, we've only got the afternoon to go.
Surely he can stay hidden for a couple more
hours?" Rafa gave Ernie an optimistic
thumbs-up.

Ernie felt a familiar knot appearing in his
stomach. A lot could go wrong if you happened

to have a dog in your pocket... They left the toilets, Ernie tapping the door frame twice for luck as he passed, then ran back to join their class.

CHAPTER 10

The Barking Boy

"So Ernie, has Rafa done a good job of showing you the ropes so far today?" Mr Mallon asked as the two boys raced into the classroom, just in time. Ernie looked at Rafa in confusion.

"R-r-ropes?" Ernie stammered. "Er..." Rafa realised that Ernie hadn't got a clue what their teacher was talking about.

"Yes, Mr Mallon, I showed him where everything was," Rafa replied for Ernie. "It's all fine — isn't it, Ernie?" He gave Ernie an exaggerated pat on the back that sent Ernie stumbling forwards. Unlike Josh, Rafa was stronger than he looked! Ernie steadied himself and nodded back enthusiastically.

"Oh yes, yes all fine, thank you." He grinned. "He showed me some very interesting places!"

"Good, good – I knew I could rely on you, Rafa," said Mr Mallon cheerfully.

Ernie hoped that he could rely on Rafa too. He followed Rafa over to their table and sat down. Maybe being at a new school might not actually be so bad... Well, as long as Swop managed to behave until home time! Ernie crossed his fingers for a few seconds for luck.

"Hurry up, settle down everyone, we have lots to do this afternoon!" Mr Mallon's loud voice filled the room. "First up — silent reading. Usual rules apply: choose a book, sit down, not a peep from anyone for the next ten minutes!"

Table by table the children selected books from their classroom book corner. Ernie chose

a book about
pets. He was
definitely
feeling calmer. He
couldn't feel any movement
in his pocket, so he was hoping that
meant Swop was asleep. Ernie imagined him all
curled up in his pocket just like he did at home
in Ernie's dad's hat. He was no doubt tired from
eating such a lovely big lunch…

Unfortunately, Ernie had relaxed a little too
soon because then it happened. His tummy
started to rumble. Not just a little, polite, not-
likely-to-bother-anyone kind of a rumble, but
a huge, growling sort of a rumble! Ernie flung
his arms around his waist, trying to squeeze
his stomach tight to stop the noises blaring out
but it was too late. His face turned hot and red
when he realised some of the children on his
table were sniggering and staring. Clemmie

loudly told them to shush and leave him alone.
Obediently they did as they were told. And the
noises stopped.

"Remember, I
said silent reading,
Clemmie," said Mr
Mallon sternly.

Ernie sighed with
relief. He held
his breath for
a moment,
hoping it was
over. Most of
the children stopped staring and quickly
returned to their books and Ernie's face slowly
cooled down. Clemmie gave him a reassuring
half-smile. He tried to smile back but it might've
looked more like he had wind. He turned
his attention back to his book, re-reading
the sentence about bearded dragons loving

raspberries, when the noises started again —
even louder this time! Ernie didn't understand
it; he knew he was hungry but he couldn't feel
his tummy rumbling at all. The embarrassment
flooded his body, filling him from his toes up to
his cheeks. It rumbled again but this time he
felt something in his pocket... He realised that it
wasn't his tummy that was rumbling and making
all the noise — it was Swop!

Swop would usually fall asleep soon after
he had eaten. And just like a proper-sized dog,
he'd often have very vivid dreams. Swop must

have been having a very exciting dream indeed just then because he was growling and woofing so loudly that all the other children on Ernie's table could hear him, but it sounded just like it was coming from Ernie's stomach. Ernie was mortified. The children on his table and the one behind — apart from Rafa and Clemmie – all started to giggle, and then the laughter spread around the classroom like chickenpox. Ernie's head started to swim and he felt like maybe he was going to faint. He wished he would — anything to stop him from becoming the class joke.

"What's so funny, Josh?" Mr Mallon said, standing up at his desk, hands firmly on hips.

"It's Ernie, Sir, he's barking. He thinks he's a dog. Sir, maybe we should call him the Incredible Barking Boy! Ha ha ha ha! Do you think he eats bones or can do tricks for a biscuit?" Josh threw his head back and laughed even harder at his own rubbish joke.

Mr Mallon sighed and signalled for Josh to calm down as he walked over to Ernie's desk. Ernie was desperately trying to wake Swop up by gently prodding his pocket with the blunt end of his pencil. Unfortunately this wasn't working and just made Swop yelp out even louder. Ernie began to panic. What if he was told to turn out his pockets? He couldn't do that.

"As much as I love dogs, and I do love dogs, Ernie, as everyone knows I have two fantastic dogs of my own. Even so, I really do NOT want a barking boy in my class!" said Mr Mallon with one eyebrow raised higher than the other, clearly confused.

Ernie jumped as an eraser hit his arm and looked up to see Rafa staring pointedly at him. He was trying to tell him something but Ernie had no idea what that could be. Had he spotted that he was poking the pocket Swop was in and worked out what was going on? Ernie was desperately hoping for one of Rafa's quick-thinking ideas. Rafa nodded seriously at Ernie, then did something that Ernie really wasn't expecting — he started barking too.

"Woof woof, yip yap, ruff, ruff," he barked.

"Woof woof, yap yip, arghh, arghh," barked Ernie too. For a split second Ernie's heart sank. Had he made a terrible mistake in trusting Rafa? Was he not the loyal friend Ernie had hoped? Was he making fun of Ernie, even

though he knew what was happening and why he was barking? Mr Mallon looked at Rafa then at Ernie. His face wasn't so much cross as stunned. Ernie couldn't help but feel a bit sorry for him. Mr Mallon had probably never had any pupils bark at him before.

"Rafa, Ernie what are you doing? What is going on?" said Mr Mallon, his face started to look less confused and more annoyed.

"Yap, yap, yap, woof WOOOOFFF! Yelllppppp, woooooooofffffff, yip yip," barked the two boys in unison.

Ernie caught Rafa's eye and his worries about his loyalties washed away. Rafa was joining in; he was supporting him and helping to keep Swop safe. Ernie hadn't been wrong about him. He was still in a terrible situation but at least he had Rafa to help, and like his Gran would say, a problem shared is a problem halved.

"Boys. Stop it now! This is a silent reading lesson. So... er... why are you pretending to be dogs?" asked Mr Mallon, shaking his head. By now most of the class were in hysterics, laughing and pointing at Ernie and Rafa.

"Yap! Woof! Yes, yaaapppp, I'm sorry Mr... Yap... Woof! Malll... yelppppp .... onnn," barked Ernie desperately.

"I just can't really... help it. Woof woof yip yap!" woofed Rafa.

"Ernie! Rafa!" snapped Mr Mallon. "That's it! One more bark, yap or growl out of either of you and I'll have to send you to the head's office! Ms Still will not be pleased to hear about this." Mr Mallon was frowning so much that his bushy eyebrows were now meeting in the middle, making them into one long hairy caterpillar. It was very clear he was not amused. "And that's enough from the rest of you too!" Mr Mallon glared around the room.

The children stopped laughing and sat up properly — they knew that look. Mr Mallon was a kind and fair teacher but he was also pretty strict. He expected the class to behave properly. The fun was most definitely over. Josh looked across the table and, once he was sure Mr Mallon couldn't see him, he mouthed, "Barking boy, barking boy!" at Ernie, then "Woof! Woof!" before panting at him with his tongue out.

Ernie felt frustrated. The things he did for Swop! He was never going to live this down. He thought back to the conversations he'd had with his dad about dogs and what kind of things they would do when they got one. He even managed a little smile to himself about how his dad would never have imagined that one day Ernie would have a miniature dog that would come to school with him, and that he'd end up barking in the classroom in front of everyone to stop it from being discovered!

Ernie sighed; this was hard. It was really hard. He was running out of energy and ideas of how to keep Swop safe. He closed his eyes for a second and wished as hard as he could that he could get through this day and arrive home safely without Swop being discovered. As if in answer to his wish, Swop made the right decision. Having woken up and heard the confusing mixture of Mr Mallon's cross voice and Ernie and Rafa's woofing, he had luckily decided that the best thing for him to do was nothing. So he curled up into a tight ball like a baby hedgehog, and tried his very best to keep still and silent.

Ernie could feel that Swop had stopped moving. He willed the little dog to stay calm.

He was already imagining Mr Mallon sharing his hilarious "barking boy" story with all the other teachers in the staffroom later, over a cup of tea and a chocolate biscuit. He couldn't even bring himself to look at Rafa. He was embarrassed that he'd got Rafa in trouble too – Ernie didn't want to put him off being his and Swop's friend before the end of the first day! Though he was very pleased that Rafa had helped him out. Ernie had a feeling Rafa was going to be a loyal friend.

As Mr Mallon walked past his desk, Ernie caught his eye and said, "I'm really very sorry, Mr Mallon, and it wasn't Rafa's fault." He was sorry he had barked at his teacher. He was also sorry that his dad was no longer around to help him get out of these scrapes. He was sorry that he had moved to London. And he was particularly sorry that Swop had ended up coming to school with him today, that he had sneaked into his lunchbox (and not forgetting that he had also ruined Gran's legendary cupcake).

"OK, Ernie," said Mr Mallon, his voice growing softer when he saw Ernie's tearful expression. "Let's draw a line under this experience. I'll just put this episode down to you being... er... overexcited about your first day here." Mr Mallon tapped Ernie's reading book and walked away, shaking his head as he went.

CHAPTER 11

The Duck Was Pushed!

"OK everyone, it's maths now and you'll be very pleased to hear that we're having the charity toy sale as promised!" said Mr Mallon. "I hope you've all remembered to bring in some pocket money to spend. You can practise using real money, give an old toy a new home and raise some cash for a great cause too. It's a win-win situation!"

He smiled broadly. He seemed to have forgotten all the barking business. There were two tables at the back of the classroom piled high with all sorts of old cuddly toys, action figures and books. A few children had offered to spend their playtimes sticking price tags on all the toys. There was a box ready for the money and Mr Mallon had a float to be used for change, so that they could spend their money and practise working out the change in their heads. There was also a notepad at the side if they needed to write down the prices.

Ernie gazed over at the sorry-looking collection of unwanted toys that were up for sale. He couldn't believe how rubbish some of them were. A plastic polar bear with red felt tip all over its face (16p), a trouser-less, one-legged soldier (7p) and even a one-eyed, one-whiskered cuddly toy cat. The miserable tabby was definitely overpriced at 30p.

"No-one's going to buy that," he thought. There were some good books, though, so maybe they would be popular.

Mr Mallon explained what they had to do. "We'll take turns to visit the sale, one table at a time. Rafa's table can start. Ernie, to get yourself focused again, why don't you take the money for your group. Make sure you check the totals carefully." Clemmie, Josh and Rafa headed off to

SCRABBLE

CLUe

PUZZLE

500

browse the toy tables. Ernie got ready to take their money.

"You have five minutes to do your shopping. And do try to add up the totals in your head as you go along," explained Mr Mallon.

"I'm good with money,"

said Clemmie. "I earn pocket money from doing lots of chores at home." She started looking through the stuff on the table, chattering away to herself as she did so. "...That's too old, that's too babyish, that's seven pence and adding sevens is sooooo boring..."

Ernie was feeling so hungry that he started to lose concentration. The more he tried to focus, the more his mind wandered. He couldn't stop thinking about all the snacks he would like to have after school. He was hungry and very aware that he had missed lunch. Suddenly something bounced off his foot, forcing him back to reality. He looked down to see a rubber duck coming to a halt next to his chair leg. As he looked up to see where it had come from, the duck was closely followed by a miniature Spiderman.

Clemmie was far too busy talking to herself to notice, but as Ernie looked at the toy table

he could see a little gap at the front and a
familiar furry shape pushing its way through.
Ernie's eyes widened in shock. The duck and
Spiderman toys hadn't just fallen – they'd
been pushed!

There was the culprit — his one and only
furry friend, Swop. The little dog was now
sitting smugly between a rag doll with a wonky
head and the one-eyed cat. His tongue was
lolling out of the side of his mouth and his eyes
had a mischievous twinkle about them as he
scanned the room. Ernie instinctively clutched
at his left trouser pocket, but
he already
knew...
his pocket
was now

definitely a dog-free zone.

Without thinking he cried out, "Swop, NO!"

Rafa turned immediately, staring at Ernie. Ernie tipped his head to the side, then opened his eyes wide at the same time, trying to will Rafa to notice Swop on the table. Rafa seemed to have no idea what Ernie was trying to tell him. Clemmie spun around to see a very flustered-looking Ernie. He clutched his hand over his mouth to stop any more words flying out. Clemmie picked up the stray Spiderman figure and smiled. Ernie was surprised by her choice. She had been nice to him a few times and had told Ernie that she had been a new girl last year, so he guessed she knew it was like not to know anyone. Maybe she had worked out that he was about to get into trouble yet again.

"Oh, sorry Ernie, that was my fault. I must have knocked him off the table, don't worry, I'll put him back." She winked at him, just a bit too obviously. She turned and looked straight at Mr Mallon, hoping this might be enough to stop him being annoyed, but it wasn't. He waved his finger sternly in Ernie's direction.

"Ernie... concentrate, please!"

Ernie watched in horror as Clemmie now moved towards Swop. Swop looked wide-eyed at Ernie. Ernie held the four fingers of his right hand smartly up to his forehead, like a salute: the sign language for "Danger". Luckily Swop saw the signal and understood immediately. He snapped to attention and stood frozen on the spot but it was too late. Clemmie had spotted him.

"Oh, look at this little dog! Where has he come from? He's soooo cute — and he still has all four legs and both of his eyes! And no one has drawn on him. Is he a key-ring? I collect key-rings to hang off my rucksack, I have eight already," cooed Clemmie, as she grabbed Swop off the table. "How much is he?"

She turned Swop upside down, looking around for a price sticker. Swop was trying hard to stay still but all the swivelling about was making him feel dizzy and his eyes were rolling a bit. Ernie held his breath as Swop held his legs up in the air, as straight and stiff as mini-breadsticks. (Ernie was so hungry, everything reminded him of food.)

"Ernie, how much is this scruffy little dog toy? I can't see a price on him anywhere, can you?" quizzed Clemmie.

"Er... um. It's 57p." He coughed and

managed to squeak out
an answer.

"Well, that is very
expensive but I have
to have him,"
Clemmie said
firmly. "I'll just
have to put the
penguin pen back."

With that she
dropped Swop into her

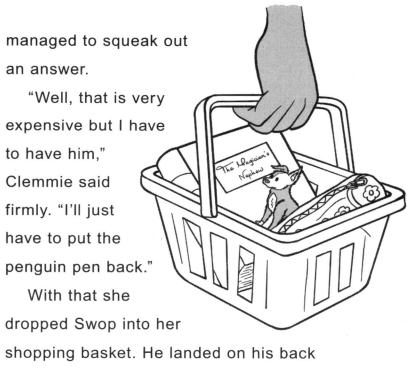

shopping basket. He landed on his back
and rolled to one side with his four legs still
stretched out straight in front of him. He looked
like he'd been frozen by a spell.

"Oh no, I don't think he can stay still for
much longer!" thought Ernie in a panic. In their
practice sessions, Swop had only managed
to hold this pose for twenty-seconds before
leaping up and snaffling his treat.

Ernie picked Swop out of Clemmie's basket, pretending to look for a price on him but really he was just turning him back the right way up. He didn't want Swop to feel sick, but before he had a chance to think what to do next, Clemmie had swiped the little dog back out of his hand and stuffed Swop into her cardigan pocket, stroking him on the head as she did so.

Ernie could see Swop was enjoying it.

He grabbed the money out of Clemmie's hand, chucked it in the till and gave her back a handful of random change. Ernie was so worried about how to get Swop back, he didn't care

103

that Mr Mallon was glaring at him.

Clemmie held out her hand and stared at her change, confused. She'd ended up with more money than she'd started with. She frowned and then sat down and got on with her maths, keeping an eye on Ernie while Ernie kept an eye on her cardigan pocket! He could see the top of Swop's head poking out of Clemmie's pocket. If anyone looked closely they would have seen the little "toy" dog's eyes moving as he looked around the room.

The only person who seemed to have noticed was Rafa. His eyes went wide as he watched Ernie sign "Stay" and "Quiet" subtly under the table to Swop until he started getting funny looks from the rest of his classmates and had to turn around and get on with being the shopkeeper. There was nothing Rafa could do to help. Ernie couldn't count properly he was so anxious (and hungry), and he kept giving everyone the wrong change, either charging them too much or too little.

Finally, his table had all made their purchases and Ernie was allowed to sit down. He hoped that Swop hadn't escaped from Clemmie's pocket. That was probably the safest place for him right now but Ernie had no idea how he was going to get Swop out of her pocket and home to his bedroom without being spotted.

CHAPTER 12

The Leak In The Library

"OK, class, it's time for your drama session in the library. Tidy your desks and we can finish this work when you get back," announced Mr Mallon. He made his way over to the classroom door. The children shuffled their books and pencil cases around and waited for the teacher to point to their table. When he did, they tucked their chairs neatly away and lined up. Except for Josh, who scraped the floor with his chair legs and made Mr Mallon frown.

Ernie just had to hope that Swop had the sense to stay hidden... He rubbed the back of his neck while thinking what to do next. Finally, Mr Mallon pointed at Ernie's table, so Ernie stood up and pushed in his chair. He couldn't see Clemmie or her cardigan pocket because she was already standing at the front. His heart was racing. Ernie took a deep breath and straightened his back. He shoved his sweaty hands deep into his empty pockets and joined the line. The line started moving. They had to walk through the main hall (full of nursery children marching around, pretending to play trumpets), and then up the stairs to the library. Rafa tried to skip up to the front to get a better view of

Clemmie but he was seen and told to go back.

The library was in the corner of the building and had two big glass windows with bookshelves lined up behind the tables. In one corner there were two faded blue beanbags that smelt musty, like old PE kits. Rafa had said that no one wanted to sit on them, although their drama teacher insisted on using them as a reward for good behaviour — that was one of the reasons this lesson was always so noisy.

As they filed in and took their seats, Ernie could just see Clemmie on the table to his right. He bent down and rolled his pencil case along the floor as if he had dropped it. He got close enough to see that her cardigan pocket still had something in it but nothing was poking out that he could identify as Swop, and it wasn't as if he could just put his hand in her pocket to check that Swop was still there. He and Rafa looked at each other. Rafa shrugged. For once, he didn't have a plan either.

"Settle down, everyone. You're all going to love this new play — it's magnificent! We will all get a chance to take a part," said Mrs Hepburn. Their drama teacher had a very loud, posh voice, as if she were performing in a theatre production all the time.

She carried on talking to them, giving them one copy of the play to read between two of

them as she went around the class. Then
Clemmie took off her cardigan and hung it on
the back of her chair. Ernie was thrilled. It gave
him the chance to sneak Swop back without her
seeing him. He put his hand up,

thinking of
a reason he needed
to move over towards
Clemmie – but before
he had the chance to ask
there was a clatter and a crash,
as a cardboard model of a rocket from a book
display about space flew off the shelf behind
Clemmie. It went over her and her partner
Esme's heads and crashed on to the table.

They both leapt up, shrieked and looked at the shelves behind them.

"Don't blame me, Miss," shouted Josh, putting his hands in the air to show how innocent he was.

Ernie got the impression that Josh was so used to being blamed (and probably for good reason) that now he just expected it, but this time it was nothing to do with him. Mrs Hepburn just ignored him.

"Girls, are you OK?" she asked.

"Yes," said Clemmie, "but none of us moved, Miss. It wasn't anyone on this table."

Mrs Hepburn nodded, apparently persuaded by Clemmie's answer, but before she could say another word, a book fell off the shelf further along and then another and another... They were flying out one after the other, pages flapping, as if they had been given magical powers and could suddenly fly. Ernie stood up

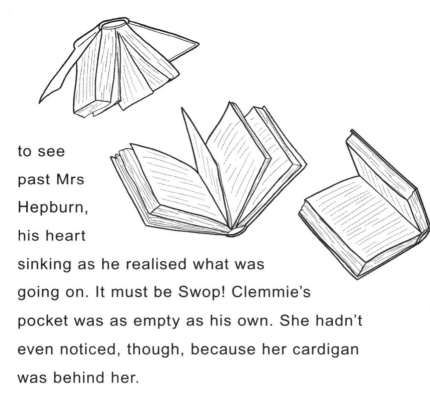

to see
past Mrs
Hepburn,
his heart
sinking as he realised what was
going on. It must be Swop! Clemmie's
pocket was as empty as his own. She hadn't
even noticed, though, because her cardigan
was behind her.

"AHHHHHHHHHHHHHHHHHH!" screeched
Esme, as a book landed on her head.

"EEEEEEKKKKKKKKKKKK!" squeaked
Anton, as another book knocked over his water
bottle. Ernie was up out of his seat as quick
as a flash. He picked up the fallen books and
checked the shelves, Rafa joining in to help, but
Swop was too fast and always one disastrous
step ahead of them.

"Ergggghhhh!" squealed Maya, as she leapt out of her seat and put her hands up to her head. She looked up at the ceiling. "Mrs Hepburn, there's, erm some water dripping on my head. The roof must have a leak!"

"Ha, it's not water it's rat weeeeeee!" called Josh.

"Nooooo, it can't be, that's disgusting!" cried Maya, jumping up and away from her chair.

"ERRRRRRRRRRR!" chorused the rest of the table.

Before Mrs Hepburn could answer, a blur

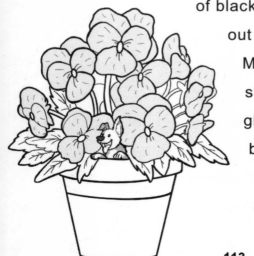

of black-and-white fur leapt out of a plant pot behind Maya, ran along the shelf, slid down a globe to the shelf below, jumped on to the floor and raced across to the door

— and straight out through it! The children who had seen the furry visitor screamed, and the children who hadn't seen it screamed even louder. Josh pointed at Maya. Ernie looked at the plant pot on the shelf above and his stomach sank. It might have been a little leak but it could also have been a little wee! A Swop-sized wee! Luckily it wasn't dog wee that Josh was imagining...

"That's so gross! You've definitely got rat wee in your hair, I CAN SEE IT!" yelled Josh with delight. Maya glared at Josh, who grinned back. Ernie

watched with horror as the smallest drip moved down Maya's hair and made a teeny plop on to the desk.

"Erggghhhhhhhhhh!" she screamed as she grabbed George's jumper off the table and started frantically rubbing her head with it, while George equally frantically tried to pull his jumper back off her. They looked like they were doing some kind of crazy static electricity experiment. Ernie leaned out of the classroom door and looked down the corridor but he was too late, Swop had gone. The door to the playground outside was ajar. He looked back at Rafa. "We need to go and follow him!" he mouthed.

Luckily, Mrs

Hepburn had half-fainted and slumped herself on the chair behind, with her head back and her feet outstretched, waving a graphic novel across her face like a fan, as she talked to herself.

"Oh dear, oh dear, a rodent, a RO–DENT has been amongst my lovely bookshelves and beautiful drama studio. There will be rat poo on the carpet, and who knows how many of the gorgeous books have been nibbled on? There could be a whole family of them living inside my Shakespeare collection. Someone go and get Mr Fellows. Please fetch Mr Fellows..."

Mr Fellows was the caretaker. Ernie's

mind was racing. He looked at Rafa. Rafa nodded, this was their chance — together they approached Mrs Hepburn with very serious faces and a plan already in place.

"Mrs Hepburn, please don't worry. Leave it to us. Just let me and Ernie go and find the caretaker and get this all sorted for you. You just rest here and take it easy. You've had a nasty shock, leave it to us," said Rafa.

Mrs Hepburn dabbed the corners of her dry eyes with a purple hankie she had pulled from her sleeve and nodded, sniffed, then nodded again, wafting her hand towards the door to give her permission. Rafa nodded and he and Ernie ran off. Rafa was proving to be pretty dynamic, thought Ernie. He seemed to just get on and do things while Ernie was still busy thinking them over. They left the library as fast as they could.

CHAPTER 13

The Fake Chicken

There was only one way to go when you left the library, so Ernie and Rafa hurried along the corridor, carefully slowing down as they passed each classroom door in case any teachers saw them running. Ernie whispered Swop's name as they went. Once they had searched the corridor with no sign of the little dog, they went out in to the main playground.

"He could be anywhere by now," Rafa said, as he glanced towards the main school gates.

"Maybe he's sniffed out some more food?" said Ernie hopefully. "Is there anywhere he would find any?"

"We could check by the chickens. There's always a bucket of food for them nearby. It's worth a look — it's only just behind the nursery fence," Rafa replied.

They ran over to the slatted wooden fence across the playground, Ernie thinking that they would have to be quick before someone asked

them what they were up to. "We are looking for the caretaker in the chicken run" wouldn't really be the best reason. As they approached the fence, Ernie and Rafa could hear little voices chattering. There were a couple of nursery children feeding the chickens and looking into the run at some chicks. There were two adults as well but they were chatting with their backs to the children and the chickens. A little boy in blue wellies ran over to the teacher and pulled her cardigan.

"Miss, Miss – there's a new baby chicken in there but it's different to all the others!"

"No, there isn't Ben," the teacher answered, without even looking at him. "Just go and feed them, we'll have to go back to class in a minute." And she peeled his clingy fingers off her cardigan.

"But there are one, two, three, four, five babies now," Ben insisted, counting on his fingers.

"No, Ben, there are definitely only four," said the other teacher firmly, before carrying on chatting. The little boy huffed and turned back to the pen, shoving himself to the front of the run, and started pointing at something.

"Look, look, he's black and white!" he shouted back at the teacher. Rafa and Ernie looked at each other as they heard this, then bent down and peered through the slats of the fence.

"Hello, Hello, Ben..." Ernie tried to get the little boy's attention, waving his fingers through

the gap, but instead a little girl came over
to him.

"Hello, why does that baby chick have a
tail?" she asked, as she came right up to the
fence. Ernie wasn't quite sure what to say back.

"I don't know. What's his tail doing?"
he asked.

"It's moving sideways and he has too many
legs." She giggled. "What is it, is it a funny kind
of guinea pig?"

"Yes, that's right, it's a very unusual kind of
Australian guinea pig," said Rafa.

Ernie was impressed that Rafa could think
of answers so fast. The little girl shrugged,
turned and went back to the run, where she
found a piece of carrot and dangled it through
the netting.

"Here little piggy, here little piggy,"
she called.

And then there he was. Ernie watched as

Swop ran straight up to the carrot stick and took it from the girl's hand. He was covered in sawdust from the chicken floor, with a couple of feathers stuck to him too. Ernie could see why she didn't realise Swop was a dog.

"Chickens and guinea pigs don't have tails or teeth like that," said the girl as she looked back suspiciously at Rafa and Ernie.

"Er, it's a very, very rare kind of guinea pig," said Rafa seriously, as Ernie nodded quickly in agreement beside him.

"That chicken is not a chicken," said a girl wearing a jumper with a big frog embroidered on the front. "It's got sticky-up ears and it is running like a big spider."

"Misssss, there's a spider!" shrieked a boy who was listening and watching what was going on from the side. He stood slightly away from them and started crying.

"Err, no I really don't think it's a spider..." said Ernie kindly to the little boy. "What colour was it?"

The little boy turned to face Ernie and stopped crying. "It was a bit black, a bit white and a bit feathery, but it's not a chicken. It's eating a carrot underneath the mummy chicken."

"It's got no wings," said another little girl, coming up to the fence to see who the boy was talking to, her long ponytail swinging.

"It's a baby peacock, I think," said Ben, nodding and approaching the fence to join the others talking to Rafa and Ernie.

One by one, the group of children came over to talk to Rafa and Ernie, their interest in

the chickens overtaken by the chance to talk to big children through the fence. Their stories became more wild too as they tried to get the interest of the big boys. The teachers were still chatting and had their backs to the small crowd forming at the fence instead of beside the chickens.

Ernie and Rafa were running out of time and ideas. They needed to get inside the run. Now all the children had moved away from it,

Ernie could see through to the chicken coop
and there, poking out from under the feathers
of the fluffiest chicken Ernie
had ever seen (and he had
lived in the countryside),
was Swop. The
little dog had his
head sticking
out and was
still happily
gnawing

away on the carrot. He looked very relaxed
under the feathery chicken. There was even
a chick nearby — all the chicks were just
ignoring him.

Before Ernie had a chance to speak to Rafa,
a harsh voice called the children away from
the fence.

"Right, what are all of you doing over there?
It's time for the next group to come in now,

so everyone back over here and line up —
and I don't want to hear any more talk about
extra chickens! I think you all need to practise
counting this afternoon!" She parted the gaggle
of children and leaned over the fence. "Oh, so
that's what you are all doing at the fence. Who
are you boys? What are you doing calling all the
children over to you?"

"Leave this to me," whispered Rafa to Ernie.

"Hello Miss, I am giving Ernest here a tour
of the school. He's new, you see, and I wanted
to show him the amazing chicken run. He loves
chickens. In fact, he loves them so much he's a
strict vegetarian!"

Ernie nodded, going along with Rafa's story.
"Oh yes, I love chickens, I really do." He wasn't
vegetarian but he'd agree to anything if it gave
him a chance to get Swop back. Before the
teacher got a chance to answer, the boys heard
their names being called behind them.

"Ernie, Rafa, there you are! I assume you're Ernie and Rafa?" A friendly looking man in overalls with a huge bunch of keys had stopped in the middle of the playground. He put down his bucket and stared over at them.

"Mrs Hepburn sent a message and said she'd sent you to find me, but that you hadn't come back and you hadn't found me either. You need to get yourselves inside before she volunteers you to spend the next two weeks after school helping me clean out the nursery toilets!" He smiled, clearly amused at the idea.

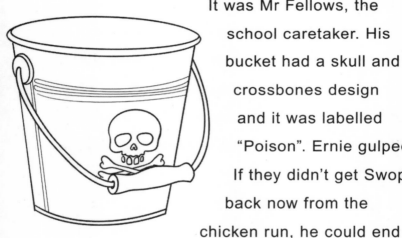

It was Mr Fellows, the school caretaker. His bucket had a skull and crossbones design and it was labelled "Poison". Ernie gulped. If they didn't get Swop back now from the chicken run, he could end up eating poison! They were so close to him, yet they could have been miles away with this fence between them. The nursery teacher was glaring at them through the fence and now the caretaker was glaring at them from the playground. They had no choice but to leave Swop where he was and head back to class.

Ernie's heart felt as heavy as his chunky new school shoes as he dragged himself towards Mr Fellows. They had been so close to catching Swop – but not close enough.

CHAPTER 14

The Rat Riot

"Welcome back, everyone, to our first assembly of the new term."

Ms Still, the head teacher, was standing in the middle of the stage in a superhero stance, legs apart and hands on her hips. The classes flowed into the hall slowly under her watchful gaze. Once they were all in, Ms Still signalled for them to sit down and they did so almost as one. "Well, I must say, you all came into the hall beautifully this afternoon. Well done, everybody," she said, smiling.

Ernie did not smile back. He had been told

that praise from the head teacher was very important. His classmates had said that they all wanted to impress her. She seemed to be looking at Ernie, though, which was making him uneasy. He was filled to the brim with worry. The worry wouldn't stay inside. It was making him fidget with his laces and squirm around. Where was Swop? He couldn't help feeling that something was about to go very, very wrong. They had almost got Swop back, if only they could have got into the nursery playground...

Ernie didn't have to wait long to be proved right about something going wrong. Ms Still had no sooner turned her back to switch on the overhead projector when a loud sob erupted from a little girl on the front row. Her shoulders were moving up and down as she cried, so much so her black plaits were jumping about in the air. A girl on her left started crying because she had been flicked straight in the eye by one. The boy on her right was leaning away so much that the side of his face was nearly flat on the floor. The little girl's teacher ran towards her.

"Whatever's the matter?" she asked, bending down and placing a reassuring hand on the girl's shoulder.

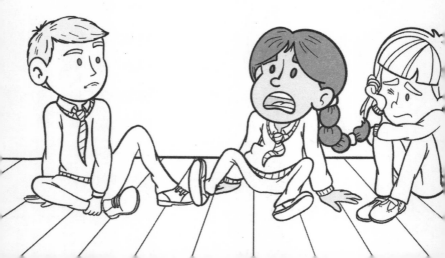

"A mole, a mole!" the child sobbed again, and she pointed sharply at the piano.

The teacher tried not to smile. "I don't think a mole would be in the school hall, dear, they live in th–"

"There!" The little girl pointed again and pulled her jumper up and over her head, hiding inside it like a hermit crab.

"It's a mouse!" shouted another small voice.

Ms Still stood, mouth agape, as a flash of fur leapt off the piano, ran around it twice and then darted under the crate of PE mats. She might have been a grown-up but Ernie thought she looked as frightened as the little girl. He stared helplessly at the chaos. He knew immediately that this was not a mole, a rat or even a mouse. Oh, Swop, how can you be so small yet cause so much trouble?

More children started shouting. Most of them hadn't actually seen anything but joined

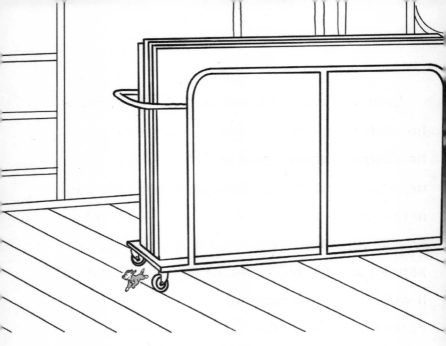

in anyway. Teachers attempted to calm their classes but in vain. Boys and girls scooted backwards on their bottoms to move away from the "rat", knocking over other children behind them. Then those children pushed back, even harder, which is when the real trouble started. Soon the whole school seemed to be rolling around on the floor or running to the door, crying, laughing or screaming.

Ms Still marched up and down the stage, shouting for calm. She grabbed a broom from the side of the stage and held it across her chest like a shield. She certainly wasn't heading anywhere in the direction of the unknown creature. As she desperately fumbled in her pockets for her PE whistle, the speedy fur ball appeared from under the mats and zig-zagged across the hall, dodging children as it went. Everyone scrambled towards the far corner, trying to get as far away as possible from the escaping "vermin".

Except Ernie, who for once knew exactly what to do!

CHAPTER 15

The Accidental Hero!

Ernie sprang into action, chasing Swop across the hall, swerving and jumping over legs and jumpers. He was trying to tackle the little dog like a rugby player would — not that he had ever played rugby but he used to pretend to watch it sometimes when it was on TV with his dad.

Thump! His first attempt ended in a miss. He ran and jumped and then dived again. Whumph! Another miss. Then, as luck would have it, Swop looked behind him as he ran, recognised Ernie, paused and thump! Ernie was on the

ground with Swop safely caught between his
two cupped hands. He couldn't believe it. He
had been the one to think quickly of a solution
and it had worked! But now what should he do?

He glanced around. Every
face he could see was
focused on him.

Ms Still blew her
whistle so hard that her
cheeks looked fit to pop.
"Wheeeeeeeeeeeeeeee
eeeeeeeeeeeeeeeeee

eeeeeeeeeeeeeeeeeeeeeeeeeeeeeeeeeeeeeeeeee
eeeeee!"

The whole hall fell silent and every face
turned from Ernie to face their head teacher.

"Bravo young man! Bravo!"

Ernie looked up from the floor where he was
shielding Swop and smiled in embarrassment.
He could feel the heat rising up his body. It
always happened when he became the centre
of attention. Ms Still was looking straight at
him and applauding! In fact, the whole school
was clapping and cheering now. He raised
his cupped hands up in acknowledgement, as
though he were showing them a trophy.

"Don't worry," he said. "It's just a... a... teeny
tiny mouse, definitely not a mole or a rat. A
frightened little field mouse. I'm going to take
him outside and let him go."

A few small children got up and started to
run towards Ernie, asking to see it. He moved

away quickly, heading for the door. Mr Mallon ran ahead and swung it open, he was grinning at Ernie too, which made a nice change, Ernie thought. The door led out to the school's nature area. Ernie bolted outside, being extra careful not to show anyone what he was actually holding. He headed for the farthest and biggest bush and quickly bent down, whispering reassurances to Swop as he slipped him out of his hand and on to the grass. Swop was panting after his sprint around the hall.

"Stay, Swop," Ernie said seriously, keeping his voice low so Mr Mallon couldn't hear him. "You have to wait here." He turned his hands palm down and moved them slightly side to side like he was smoothing something down, before changing and moving them gently up and down a little — they were the signs for "Settle down" and "Stay". "I'll collect you after school. Wait here in this bush, but stay hidden. I promise I'll

be back very soon with a special treat for you."

They had only ever practised this settle-and-stay routine for around fifteen minutes so far. Ernie needed to buy some time, get back to the classroom and find his rucksack. He had another plan. He was couldn't believe it but he was actually fizzing with confidence! Swop seemed to understand and was calmed by Ernie's instructions, so he lay down and caught his breath as he settled under the bush. Ernie jumped as he felt two firm hands land on his shoulders. It was Mr Mallon, standing behind him.

"Well, Ernie, you seem to have saved the

day! How brave of you to catch that little fella. What was it? A mouse, eh? Clever thinking, young man. You have saved the day and saved the mouse!" Ernie flushed red, from the nape of his neck right to the tips of his ears.

"Yes, Mr Mallon," he nodded, gulping. "It was just a tiny field mouse, I think, small and fluffy... It's gone now, it ran far, far away," he explained, without meeting his teacher's eye. Mr Mallon smiled approvingly and steered Ernie back towards the hall, where everyone was now back in their original places. The head teacher had straightened her glasses and was smiling again.

"Come up here," she said, beckoning Ernie onto the stage. Reluctantly he clambered up to join her. He would much rather have gone back to class without a fuss.

"Children, we need to give Ernie here a round of applause. It's his first day at Little Kings and he has certainly made sure everyone knows who he is!" Ms Still chuckled and patted Ernie on the back, a little bit too hard. "Our furry visitor is also back where he belongs, outside. It's a good moment to remember that no one must ever hurt any wildlife, however scared we are. They have as much right to be here as us. Isn't that right, children?"

"Yes, Ms Still," the children chorused in sing-song voices.

"Now, everyone needs to go back to their classrooms. Assembly is over." She had her usual head teacher voice back and the children were now all under control. Ernie forced a quick smile, thanked Ms Still, then headed back to his class with the others, pleased he'd averted a near disaster and probably stopped Swop from being flattened by a broom.

"I think you should go and wash your hands first, Ernie," suggested Mr Mallon.

Ernie agreed, especially as it also gave him the perfect opportunity to carry out the next piece of his plan. He grabbed his water bottle from his desk then walked to the door. As soon as it shut behind him, he rushed down the corridor, busy rummaging about in his coat pocket. He was sure he had a whole dog chew in there. He usually broke them up into tiny pieces for Swop and a regular-sized one normally lasted a week. Today he needed a whole one if he was going to persuade Swop to stay in one place and keep safe until the bell rang and they could both go home. His school bag was in the locked cupboard back in the classroom so he couldn't even hide him in there.

Ernie headed back towards the nature area and (hopefully) Swop. It was risky — he could easily be spotted — and he didn't have a back-up plan but there was no way he could leave Swop there for another hour or so without something to do. He bent down by the bush and called quietly to the little dog.

Nothing.

He called Swop's name a little louder.

Still nothing.

Trying not to panic, he tried a third time, and finally heard a reassuring rustle in the undergrowth. Ernie's body relaxed and he breathed out in a great rush.

"Ah there you are, Swop, good boy! I'm really sorry but you'll have to stay here for just a little bit longer." Swop was pleased to see his best friend and wanted to run up his body to lick his face. Ernie had to be firm. He stroked the little dog and put him back on the ground, still crouching so no one would see him. Then he unscrewed the lid of his water bottle and used it as a water bowl. Swop stuck his head straight in and quickly lapped up every drop. Thankfully, he was tired out. Ernie reached in to his pocket

for the chew stick, which was almost twice as long as Swop. He waved it in front of the little dog with a flourish and smiled.

"This should keep you going for the rest of the afternoon. We only have one more lesson to go so it's not that long..." said Ernie as he lay it down in front of Swop, whose tongue was already hanging out in anticipation. He signed "Wait, wait" to him, and "Yip, yip," agreed Swop, bowing down, ready to pounce on the treat as soon as it was given to him.

Ernie signed "Go" and Swop went, opening his tiny jaws as wide as he could to get a grip on the super-sized treat. Ernie waited a moment for Swop's excitement to calm, then caught the little dog's eye and signed "Settle" and "Stay" again. He repeated the signs a few times but he still didn't feel confident that Swop was concentrating, he was still panting from racing around the hall. He waited for a moment until

Swop settled down and started to gnaw at the chew with his tiny teeth, and just then a genius idea popped in to his head.

He bent down, undid one shoelace and removed his heavy school shoe, wobbling as he did so, until he fell back on to the tarmac. Swop was so engrossed in his feast that didn't even look

up. Ernie pulled off his sock and sniffed it —
hmm, not quite smelly enough. So he rubbed
his foot and in between his toes with the sock
and sniffed it again. Yes, definitely a strong
whiff of foot. Dogs have a far better sense of
smell than humans so he knew Swop would
recognise that this was Ernie's smell and
hopefully that would help him settle. He shaped
the sock into a makeshift bed and gently lifted
Swop onto it, laying the chew stick carefully in
front of him.

"There you go, now stay, OK?" He signed
and said, "Stay!" with as much authority as he
could muster. He even moved his head to one
side, opening one eye a little wider than the
other, giving Swop his version of a stern
mum look.

Swop looked at him with his bright, conker-
coloured eyes and held his gaze for a split
second before getting back to chewing. Ernie

tapped the bush twice for luck and scarpered back to class, hoping he hadn't taken too long. This first day was becoming more of a rollercoaster than he could ever have imagined. At least there wasn't that much time left before he (and Swop) could go home...

CHAPTER 16

The School Trip!

The rest of the afternoon was thankfully uneventful, apart from having to "fake help" Clemmie look for the lost puppy key-ring. Ernie volunteered to help her look around the hall, as Mr Mallon had suggested it might have fallen out of her pocket when they were all trying to avoid the rat in assembly. Ernie did feel a bit guilty as Clemmie was really disappointed to have lost it, so much so that Mr Mallon allowed her to choose two toys free of charge from the toy table, which seemed to cheer her up. It cheered up Ernie too, as she had been really kind to him and he didn't like tricking her. Especially as she kept thanking him for helping her!

Soon it was time for everyone to tidy up in preparation for going home. It had definitely been a busy day for Ernie and he was desperate to collect Swop and leave. His tiny, satsuma-sized dog may have barked at his teacher and squirted yoghurt over Rafa, he may have been mistaken for a key-ring and got the head teacher thinking her school had a rodent invasion — but at least he hadn't been discovered. The day would end just fine, as long as Swop was still in that bush. Then Ernie could get back to doing what he loved best: hanging out with Swop at home. Ernie slumped down on the carpet with the rest of his class. He stared at his new hard and uncomfortable leather shoes, their tell-tale splodges of yoghurt now just dried faint pink dots. He rubbed his bare ankle and hoped no one had noticed that he was only wearing one sock. Mr Mallon clapped his hands together loudly to get the class's attention.

"Now, children, Ernie has finished his first day at this school, and starting a new school is always difficult even without the adventures he's had," he said, smiling. "So, please give him a Little Kings round of applause. And remember that next week is our first school trip of the year — so it will be an exciting week for all of you!"

The class cheered, and Ernie looked up. He didn't know about the trip.

153

Before he
had the chance to
daydream about where
they might be going,
Clemmie whispered
across to him. "It's to the Natural History
Museum. It's a brilliant trip." She grinned, and
Ernie grinned back. Surely it couldn't be true?
He'd never been this lucky. He'd never so much
as won a raffle. How could his favourite place
on earth, the Natural History Museum, be the
destination of the first trip at his new school?
He was speechless and desperate to hear what
else Mr Mallon had to say.

"We will of course need parent helpers, as
always, so I will give you these letters to take
home. Please send back your permission slips

and also the phone numbers of any parents or carers who are able to join us. And let's hope next week will be easier for you, eh, Ernie? Anyone willing to help Ernie out and be his partner on Monday, and perhaps be in his group for the trip too?"

Ernie slumped even lower in his seat. He wasn't sure how much more humiliation he could take. It was only a few hours ago that he had been barking!

"I will," said a voice beside him. Ernie looked  up and Rafa flashed him a broad grin.

"Me too," offered Clemmie, her hand straight up in the air.

"That's brilliant, Rafa," said Mr Mallon. "And thank you, Clemmie. You can both be in his trip group, then. Is that OK with you, Ernie?"

Ernie nodded and managed a small but very real smile.

"OK, right then. Let me see who is ready to go. If I say your initial then you can head off, but listen carefully as it's not in any order! If your first name begins with an L, off you go," said Mr Mallon. Lila and Lenny stood up and left the room.

Ernie was itching to go, too. It seemed like a strange way to do it. Rs went next, so Rafa and Ronnie gathered their things and made for the door.

"Hey Ernie, could you just ask your mum to leave the yoghurt out of your packed lunch on trip day?" whispered Rafa as he passed.

"Ha! Good idea!" said Ernie, laughing.

He sat there patiently as pupil after pupil had

their initial called out and left the room. Finally he heard Mr Mallon say, "Now, any children whose name begins with an E can go next." Ernie, Esme and Eddie stood up and went to grab their rucksacks and lunchboxes as quickly as they could. Ernie did an awkward wave to Clemmie and then headed for the door. He put on his coat and followed the others across the

playground, looking for his gran as he went.

He spotted her waiting under the

verandah. She was chatting to

a few other

parents

already.

Ernie cringed, wondering what she could possibly have to talk about with people she didn't know. He would never understand how people could just strike up conversations with strangers. She saw him and waved, so he ran over to her.

"Hello my love, all OK?" Gran asked, as she reached across to ruffle his hair. Ernie leaned sideways and instinctively pushed his hair back to where it was.

"Yes, great thanks." He crossed his fingers behind his back. "I just need to do one thing before we go, I'll be back in a minute..." He dropped his lunchbox at

Gran's feet and bolted off, leaving her looking confused.

He ran in the opposite direction to the rest of the children from his year, back to the bushes. For a second he had to look around him and make sure he was in the right place, it was all still very new to him. His heart was pounding so loudly in his ears that he looked around to see if anyone else could hear it too. He'd spent half his birthday money on cheese and dog treats to train Swop – now was the time to see if that was time and money well spent. Would Swop still be there? Had all his hours of training paid off? Or had he lost him forever?

CHAPTER 17

🐾

The Unwelcome Friend

Keeping everything crossed, Ernie bent down by the bush where he'd left Swop. Ernie's whole body was tightly coiled like a spring, desperately willing the little dog to be there.

"Swop, you can come out now," he whispered.

At the sound of Ernie's voice, a couple of tiny ears popped out of a pile of leaves, followed by a little body covered from head to paw in dirt. The chew stick was lying across Ernie's wet, muddy sock, and looking a little worse for wear. Clearly Swop had been busy.

The plan had worked! Ernie felt a little swell of pride. Knowing what made Swop happy made him happy too, despite the hassle the pup had caused him today.

Smiling, Ernie held out his hand and Swop ran over to him and leapt on to his familiar warm palm. Ernie scooped him up, kissed his tiny mucky head and popped him into the top of his rucksack. He left the zip a little undone to let in some air, then ran back to Gran, excited to set off home. He stood still for a second when he caught sight of her again. She was having a very intense conversation with Josh and Josh's mum. What was she thinking? Ernie approached them slowly, avoiding eye contact with anyone, though he could see Josh nodding in agreement with Gran.

"Ernie, I've just met your lovely new classmate, Josh," said Gran, beaming. "And I've told him all about how nervous you were about starting school and how you can't wait to make some new friends." Ernie's face flushed as red as Gran's shoes, but Granny wasn't finished yet. "So Josh said he'd love to come to tea and have a play after school one day next week. Wouldn't that be nice, Ernie?"

Josh flashed him a sly grin and coughed, muttering "Woof woof" under his breath — just loud enough that Ernie could hear him but the adults couldn't. It didn't look like Ernie had any choice in the matter, so he just nodded and kept his mouth firmly shut.

"That's settled then. We'll sort out a date soon to get them together. It's been lovely meeting you, Harriet, and your lovely boy Josh, of course." Gran smiled and so did Josh's mum. In fact, Josh's mum looked more pleased than anyone.

"I can't imagine she's ever heard the words 'lovely' and 'Josh' in the same sentence before," thought Ernie.

"Bye, Ernie, maybe see you in the bark, sorry, I meant the park!" Josh said, waving and laughing as he walked away. Ernie grabbed his Gran's coat sleeve and steered her towards the school gates.

"Ernie Targett, what's got into you?" she said confused, pulling her arm away. "I was helping you make a new friend there! He seemed like a lovely young man, and his mum was very keen to get you both together."

Wanting to change the subject because he didn't want to hurt Gran's feelings, and it was too complicated to explain anyway, Ernie turned his attention back to the only other thing on his mind at the moment: food.

"Sorry, but I'm starving, Gran, I can't concentrate. I don't suppose you've got a snack in your bag for me, have you?" Ernie smiled at her innocently.

"You can't be hungry after that monster packed lunch your mum made you! You must have had a busy day!" Gran laughed as she foraged around in her oversized handbag to get Ernie a rather bashed-up banana.

"It was a surprising day. It was very busy, Gran, it really was," sighed Ernie, as he peeled the banana and squashed it into his mouth in one quick movement. His mouth was so full his lips could hardly meet. Gran watched him but didn't say a word. Ernie loved that she didn't tell him to slow down. Ernie smiled (as best he could) and slipped his hand into hers. Then, just as quickly, he remembered where he was and removed it again immediately, bending down pretending to fiddle with his shoelace instead. He looked around to see if anyone had noticed.

Mr Mallon was right, tomorrow should be easier. And looking on the bright side, he'd already made a new friend, maybe even two if you counted Clemmie (not Josh). And unbelievably they were going to the Natural History Museum next Friday!

CHAPTER 18

🐾

Home Sweet Home

Ernie shuddered with relief as he slammed the front door behind him, shutting out the street and all the drama from his first day at his new school — but he did it just a little too hard. He let out a sigh and the two actions together were so loud that Gran turned around and stared at him.

"What's wrong, Ernie, are you OK? Your first day wasn't so bad, was it?" she asked, her eyes suddenly full of concern.

"No, I'm just relieved it's over," Ernie replied brightly.

"Me too. You've done so well, Ernie, I'm so proud of you, and I know your dad would have been too," said Gran seriously. Her shoulders sank slightly at the mention of her son but her smile didn't change. He could see she meant every word.

"I just know you'll be happy there once you settle in properly. Now, you go on upstairs and get changed, put your shirt in the washing basket and then you can play until tea's ready. Ivy will be home soon — she texted to say she has just got on the bus. Your mum won't be that long either. She's going to try and come home a bit early from the surgery today. I can't believe she's finally back at work doing what she loves. Anyone who has your mum for their doctor is pretty lucky, I can tell you!"

Ernie nodded. He knew that was true. He was proud of Mum too. Hopefully she would be a bit tired as well and he would get some time to hang out with Swop undisturbed. He carefully placed his bag on the floor and wriggled out of his coat. Gran hung up her coat on a hook in the hall and bustled off to the kitchen. Ernie knew his gran was happy that they had moved so close to her, so she was making a big effort to help look after them. Her flat was only a five-minute walk away from this new house so it was going to be very easy for her to be involved. She was going to do Ernie's school pick-ups while his mum was working or until Ernie could persuade her he could find his own way home.

He was hoping that wouldn't take too long. Apart from the pick-ups, Ernie had to admit it was really good having Gran around — and not just because she was so much better than Mum at baking!

He threw his coat over the banister and used his feet to lever off his new shoes without undoing the laces. Grabbing his school bag, he bounded up the stairs two at a time. This new house was smaller but taller than his last one, so at the top of stairs he turned a sharp left and left again to head up to best room in the house — his bedroom in

the attic. He had to admit he quite liked looking
out over the rooftops, and the news of the
school trip had made him more positive and
optimistic than he was expecting. He shut his
door firmly behind him, put his rucksack on his
bed. Then he called Swop.

"Come, Swop! Come!"

As he watched, the top of his rucksack opened slightly, then the flap flipped and a little fluffy head popped out, followed swiftly by an even fluffier body. Ernie gave a thumbs-up and Swop half-sprinted, half-slid down the side of the rucksack, bumping on to the quilt. As Swop shook his fur, a few red pencil shavings flew off (one of the downsides of hiding in a school bag).

"We're home, Swop!" said Ernie. "My first day is finally over, or should I say our first day? It wasn't quite how I imagined it would be, but next week will be fantastic, as I'm going to the Natural History Museum! My dad and I used to spend whole days there together."

Swop put his head on one side and looked up excitedly at Ernie. Guessing what Swop was thinking, Ernie answered his look. "No, Swop, you can't come! I know you would love it too but there's just no way, I'm afraid — today has been just about as much adventure as I can cope with!"

Swop cocked his head to one side, looking straight at Ernie before heading off towards his shoebox to play. Ernie imagined he was trying to say, "I know, I know, I promise to stay at home and be good," although he also imagined it could

have easily have been, "Well we'll see about that!" Ernie smiled to himself. He would worry about that next week. For now he was just happy they were home.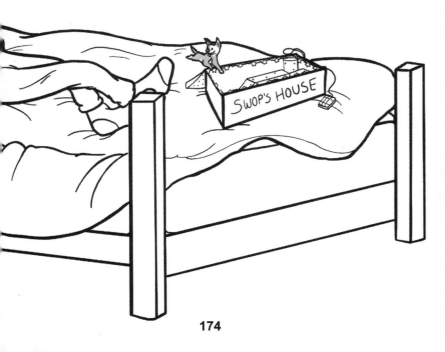

Try using Ernie's sign language poster to see if you can work out these words...

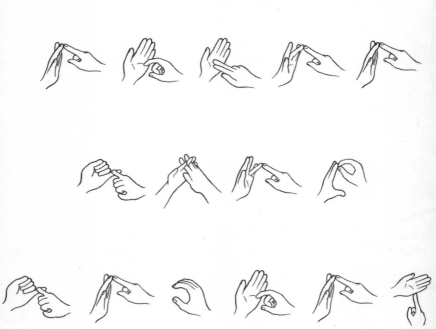

Now try finger spelling your own name using Ernie's poster?

ERNIE'S GUIDE TO SIGNING THE ALPHABET

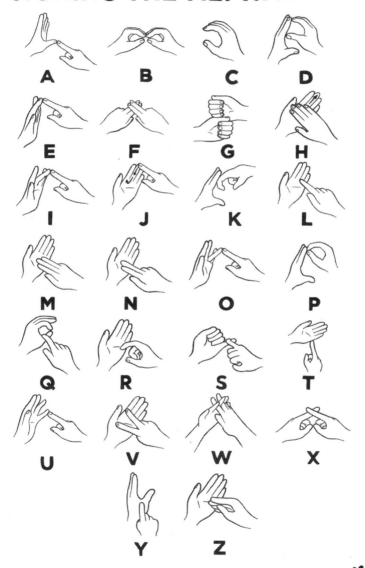

British Sign Language (BSL)

Acknowledgements

The Ai creative team (especially Finbar
Lenahan, Fabio Gois and Hazel Thomson)
who have helped me to bring my ideas to
life. They have been so wonderfully creative
and extremely patient, which means I have
ended up with a book I am so proud of. Clara
Vulliamy, who has been a fabulous mentor,
a lovely friend and for always being such a
force for all things good! My tutor Catherine
Johnson at Curtis Brown Creative, who helped
to steer me in the right direction. Faye Bird for
all the fabulous hours we have spent in coffee

shops across London, discussing books and writing and schools and kids and everything and anything... Jenny Willetts both for being my lovely friend and also for immediately answering my random text questions, day and night. Hilary Delamere for the time she gave me and her invaluable advice. Karen Ball for her fantastic brainstorming sessions! Laura Ireland for the all the different versions of Swop before we eventually got him right. Lisa Thompson for being so kind and answering all my questions. Sharon Beck for willingly listening to all of my book plans, over and over and over again. Venetia Gosling, who has been such a brilliant editor, giving me such thoughtful, practical feedback and for pushing me over the finishing line.

Mum for all the hundreds of times she took me to the library after school and then back again! Dad for all your ingenious ideas, and

for selling the book to everyone you know —
before I had even finished it! Sam, my brother,
and all the fantastic children in his classes at
Kingsthorpe Grove Primary School, for letting
me try out so many Ernie and Swop ideas.

Anthony, my husband, for humbly suggesting
I refer to him as "the wind beneath my wings"
and for never failing to tell me I could/should/
would actually finish this book. My children:
Louis, you've encouraged me to focus my work
on the things I love most (just with less heavy
metal and sewing). Madalena, your creative flair
and eye for detail never fails to impress me.
This book is so much better for it. Aubrey, you
helped me make sure the book had realistic
children's voices, and despite being asked
over and over again, you were always so
patient and encouraging.

Thank you for choosing Brilliant Monsters Books.

We want our books to be recognised as being both accessible and inclusive. We also hope to promote empathy and kindness wherever we can.

Our layouts are designed to be easily read and we use dyslexic friendly fonts as standard.

You can get in touch with us here:

✉ bmbooks@icloud.com

⬜ @BrilliantMonstersBooks

🐦 @Monsterscantalk

f Brilliant Monsters